THE SILVER MOUNTAIN

DREAMS OF LOVE

THE SILVER MOUNTAIN
DREAMS OF LOVE

Rufus Yates
Illustrated by Tyler Strouth, Kami Craft, and Rufus Yates

The Silver Mountain Dreams of Love
Copyright © 2019 by Rufus Yates

Library of Congress Control Number: 2019918031
ISBN-13:   Paperback: 978-1-950073-97-9
            ePub: 978-1-950073-98-6

Fiction / Romance / Autobiography

All rights reserved. No part of this publication may be reproduced, distributed, or transmitted in any form or by any means, including photocopying, recording, or other electronic or mechanical methods, without the prior written permission of the publisher or author, except in the case of brief quotations embodied in critical reviews and certain other noncommercial uses permitted by copyright law.

Although every precaution has been taken to verify the accuracy of the information contained herein, the author and publisher assume no responsibility for any errors or omissions. No liability is assumed for damages that may result from the use of information contained within.

Printed in the United States of America

GoToPublish LLC
1-888-337-1724
www.gotopublish.com
info@gotopublish.com

Well Mom didn't have to come after us last night, I got Linda, Josh and Emily home and still got to the house in time to eat some delicious apple pie with Pa before going to bed. We had to get ready for church the next morning and boy has it been a long weekend.

Reverend Wells had a special sermon for us this morning, he told us about the rich man having a harder time getting into Heaven and how It's better to be poor and humble. I got to thinking about that and the silver mine we found. I figured as long as we use the silver to help our neighbors and friends that should be doing a good deed. Pa agreed with me and so did Mom so that's good enough for me.

We stopped by Uncle Fred's place on the way home from church to take him to our house for supper, and to my surprise he was ready to go and he seemed to be looking forward to it. I think he got a taste of Moms cooking last Sunday and liked it, I don't think he's been eating too good for some time now, he's way too skinny, I'm just glad to have him around he reminds me a lot of Mom, they both have a calming nature, they don't get excited about anything and their really quiet.

We started out cutting our firewood close to our house years ago and over time we've had to go further and further out, now we're almost out of sight from our house so it takes a little longer to get a load each time. With four of us cutting and loading it don't take too long though, Me and Bobby, Pa and Uncle Fred got a load in no time this morning.

When we got back home Mom warmed up some food for us Pa said Grace and then Uncle Fred began telling us some more stories from the old days while we ate. We had some chicken and dumplings, Biscuits and fried apple pies for dessert. Pa tried to get Uncle Fred to stay the night but he needed to feed his live- stock. The moon was shining bright so he should be able to see the road fairly good.

After all that wood cutting and loading and stacking, Moms chicken and dumplings made it easy to fall asleep, Bobby was out, before his head hit the pillow, didn't take me long either.

Our pumpkins will be ready soon we put out two acres this year, it's the first time we tried raising pumpkins, Asa said if we raised em he would sell em. I think most of them are already sold we should make a good profit this year.

Some critter tried to get in the barn last night, the tracks look like a cat, a pretty big one, Pa said most likely a bobcat they've been seen around here lately.

Me and Josh are going to stay in the barn loft tonight and try to get that cat before it gets to Bessie our best milk cow or one of our new calves.

Mom packed us some ham and taters and some biscuits and couple pieces of pumpkin pie, she knew we would get hungry. Josh brought his dads Winchester rifle in case our traps didn't work, we set three varmint traps, one at the barn entrance so the cat will have to push on the door to get in, and that door squeaks some kind of bad, I know Ralph will hear it if we don't, and the two other traps we put near the back door.

I climbed up the loft ladder first and Josh handed me the gun while he climbed up. We piled up some hay for our beds and settled down for the night, it was almost dark and still no sign of a cat.

Josh was hungry of course so we ate while we waited on the varmint.

Josh said he had been feeling sick ever since the big festival last month, he thought maybe he'd caught something. He said it really didn't hurt like a pain, it was more like an inside kind of ache, and he feels it mostly when he thinks about Lucy. He said he can't stop thinking about her.

I told him not to feel too bad that's how I feel about Linda it was a heart ache not A hurting pain. Nobody ever took the time to tell us how it feels to be in love but I reckon that must be our ailment.

"Shh. Josh whispered hear that?"

"I hear Ralph growling." I said.

Ralph can smell a cat, fox or coon a half a mile away and he's got the scent of something.

"Be quiet and hold on to Ralph." I told Josh.

It wasn't long before squeeak! The barn door opened it was too dark now to see anything, then there goes Ralph, Josh couldn't hold him, so he took off down the feed Shoot like a bolt of lightning and Josh was right on his heels. If Ralph gets in one of them trap's he'll be hurt, I thought. I grabbed the lantern and headed down the Shoot after em.

I could hear something scuffing around and Bessie was kicking the sides of the stall and mooing and her bell was ringing like the teacher ringing her school bell when the school is on fire.

"Josh where you at?" I yelled. I guess he couldn't hear me for all the noise going on, I could hear a cat squealing and Ralph growling "Shoot that cat!" I yelled to Josh about that time I heard a snaap! I could hear the cat screaming some kind of awful.

"We got it Will. bring the light over here." Josh yells.

I made my way over to the stall and Josh had a good hold on Ralph this time but he wanted to get to that cat, and sure enough the cat's front leg was in the trap and it was almost cut clean off.

"looks like a lynx to me. Is Ralph o k?" I asked Josh.

"I think so, I almost felt sorry for that cat though." Josh said.

We stood there looking at the suffering cat with a feeling of satisfaction knowing we won this small battle.

"Well might as well shoot it", I said. "let me get Bessie out of the way first."

Pa heard the shot and came running out to the barn with his shotgun.

"Looks like you got it, is everybody o k?" he asked

"Yeah I think so Bessie is a little worked up but she'll be all right." I said.

"That's a good size cat, good job guys, let's hang it over the gate for tonight and we'll skin it in the morning."

Josh hung the lynx on the back gate behind the barn as a warning to any others varmints and came back to the loft with Ralph close behind him.

"Looks like Ralph might have some scratches on his face better check him good. A cats scratch hurts worse than any cut I know of, for some reason, they must have some kind of poison in their claws or something.

Let's get to bed it'll be daylight soon." I told Josh

It seems like every night my dreams are about Linda, I guess that's what they call love, if it aint I don't know what is.

"Will, you think anymore cats will come back tonight?" Josh asked.

"I hope not that was enough excitement for one night. good night Josh."

"Good night Will."

Alarm clocks are for city folk and we have our own, it's called OLe Red, OLe Red was a rooster, he had to be as old as me seems like he's always been here. He never missed a wake-up crowing, and you could set your clock by him to.

Seems like I just closed my eyes and there goes Ole Red crowing like he's a young rooster, he must have seen the sun coming up on the other side of the mountain cause it's still dark here, Or maybe he just smells Moms bacon like I do, you don't think chickens like bacon do you?

Mom already had a good start on breakfast, me and Josh gathered some eggs and got some wood for the stove then washed our hands and went to the kitchen where the smell was coming from.

"I Hear you boys got that cat, Lord I'm so glad I don't know what we would do if something happened to Bessie." Mom said, I got some strawberries cooked for your dessert."

"Yeah we got lucky Mom, we didn't get hurt but Ralph got some scratches on his face." I told her.

"We'll put some of that store- bought liniment on him after breakfast It will help him heal." she said.

Mom still had some of them good apples frying too, you just put some fresh home- made butter on em and let it melt some then dab it on a good hot biscuit hmm. The strawberries you just put them on your biscuits like gravy both are a little piece of heaven Pa says and I think he's right.

Bacon, eggs and brown gravy that's the way we eat most ever morning now days.

I remember many times we had potatoes three times a day and only potatoes. there's lots of different ways to fix em and they're real filling but a fellow gets tired of potatoes every meal. These days we got plenty meat and vegetables, it's a lot of hard work but it sure is worth it, all the plowing and planting and harvesting, It's our way of life. We raise crops to feed the animals we need for meat and we sell some crops to get supplies that we need from the store.

Pa says if you work hard enough for something it'll come to you, if it don't then work harder.

I believe finding the silver mine was just a reward for all the hard work and all the hard times we've been through.

We try not to take advantage of our good luck and use the silver for everyone that needs help.

Pa wants to make another trip to the mine come spring, by then we may have the ownership papers to the land, so we can stake our claim legally.

Bobby has been helping out at Asa's store ever since Asa got kicked by a mule he traded for, doc said it'll be a spell before he's able to walk again if he ever does, I was going to help him with the store but I'm needed at home more me being the oldest. I get to see Linda most every weekend now any way we're getting really close I think we'll be getting married soon, I done asked her a while back she was as happy as I was.

Bobby has Emily to help him in the store, they're pretty serious too. Pa wants us all to wait a while to get married but me and Linda got our sights set on this year, maybe Christmas.

Asa has a spare room he said we could use until we get our own place, and he's at the store most of the time anyway, we can help him till he gets better anyways.

It's funny how fast everything goes when you grow up. That's what Pa says all the time. There's a lot of things happened this year a lot of good things, and I thank the Good Lord for them every day.

I think Josh and Lucy will be getting hitched soon too, that is if Pa don't try to talk em out of it. Lucy is fifteen the same age Mom was when her and Pa got married so he can't use the age thing for an excuse. The pumpkins are looking good, we'll have a good crop for our first time planting em, we'll lose some to critters but that's to be expected.

Pa got some guineas to help guard the pumpkins, they're like little chickens but they make one heck of a racket when they hear something, they usually run most critters off.

This weekend is Halloween we're going to have a bonfire party at our place on Saturday there should be lots of friends and neighbors over. We got to take two loads of pumpkins to Asa's tomorrow the rest will be picked up by some company from Boise. At least we don't have to load them.

I been thinking about that piece of land where I planted the potatoes last year, how rich the soil was and the river was close by too and the mine is not that far away. It would make a good place for a farm for me and Linda I believe.

Mom's having last of the garden for supper tonight, it's just like it sounds all the leftover vegetables from the garden mixed together, it's really good with some ham hocks in it.

You can feel the change in the weather the air is getting colder every day, It's a pretty time of year with all the different colors and it's not too hot and not too cold. But this season don't last long enough though, It is good weather to hold your girl under the moonlight in front of a nice warm fire. Hopefully we'll be doing that tomorrow night. Me and josh and Bobby are taking the girls down to Millers Grove for the evening, just a little star gazing and socializing before it gets too cold, we'll take the Fancy coach that way if It rain's we can still go, the coach has a top.

Me and Pa got up early this morning we've got to make two trips to Asa's with pumpkins, we've got to get done early so we can go courting later.

Moms got some country ham, gravy and biscuits with fresh eggs and sweet potatoes with honey on them for dessert, It's hard to put in a good day's work without a good breakfast they tell me.

The fields still have dew on them this morning but it's a good day to work in the pumpkin patch.

We got one load by ten o'clock then set off for town, we stopped to pick Josh up on the way to the store and his sister Emily wanted to ride along too.

Asa and Bobby were ready and waiting on us when we got there and they had an empty wagon ready for us to take back.

I didn't see Linda anywhere, Asa said her and Lucy was working on the spare room at the house so we dropped Emily off and went on back to get another load.

With three of us loading pumpkins we got done pretty fast we left a few good one's in the field for another day or two they'll be just right for pies and decorating for the party, and the rest belongs to Boise Produce Company.

Pa let me and Josh take this load to the store we dropped him off at the house and went on to the store, we just had to swap wagons ours was ready to go when we got there.

Lucy and Emily had to get cleaned up for tonight so they rode back with us, I dropped Josh and Emily off and me and Lucy went on home.

I had time for a little nap before I had to get ready for our date and Mom promised to get me up if I over slept. I don't remember my head touching the pillow but I guess it did.

Me and Bobby and Sis ate supper then loaded the Fancy Coach and headed to Josh's house.

It was a little cloudy out but the rain wasn't going to stop us, we had a roof over our heads and food that Mom fixed for us.

We stopped and got Josh and Emily and headed to Linda's, she had to show me the room she was fixing up before we left, and it looked really good, looks like they worked really hard on it.

We got Asa all settled in and then we headed to Millers Grove, it's only about five miles or so from the store but it's never crowded, It's a nice place for sparking.

Linda looked prettier than all the silver in the world, I keep forgetting just how pretty she is and how lucky I am.

Asa gave us some sausages he said just put em on a stick and hold em in the fire, he said they were really good.

Well the rain held off and we set up a good spot for the fire, we got some logs for seats, and hung up some lanterns on some nearby tree branches. While the girls warmed the food up me and Josh went for firewood.

Josh wanted some advice on kissing, he wanted to know whether he should open his mouth or not and if it's o k to touch tongues. I told him we had plenty of food to eat and he didn't need to eat my little sister, I know how your always hungry. He looked at me with a funny look.

We had some ham sandwiches, and them sausages were the best I ever had, we all liked em.

The moon was shining bright through the clouds and it was chilly, we got some blankets out of the coach and snuggled up around the fire. I don't remember looking up too much after that, I was too busy looking into Linda's eyes the prettiest green you ever did see and they sparkled like the stars in the sky, I ran my fingers through her auburn hair as she kissed me for the longest time ever.

I looked over at Josh and Lucy a couple times and she was still there so I guess he didn't eat her.

And just that quick it was time to get home already, time flies when you're having fun as Pa always says.

We drew straws to see who would drive back, Josh got the short one. We gave him and Lucy a nice warm home-made quilt and they were just fine, Me and Linda took the back seat and let Bobby and Emily have the other.

I asked Linda what she thought about us building a house out west where I planted the potatoes last year. She said as long as we're together, that's all that matters but she would have to take care of her Pa until he got better. That's why she was fixing the room up for us to live in until we could get our own place and get her Pa on his feet again.

Mom and Pa liked the sausages too they asked me to get the recipe, I told them Asa bought em from some salesman I don't know If he can even get the recipe but I'll ask him.

It's not every Sunday that a new preacher comes to church way out here but this one was a good one. He had the whole church laughing, telling stories about Jonah and the whale and the whale getting an upset stomach and spitting Jonah back out into the sea. He had all kinds of funny ways to tell about the Bible so everyone could understand, sometimes it gets hard to figure out what all them words mean, for me anyway.

I think most everybody liked his sermon of course there's always some stuffy old lady or two that thinks it's a sin to laugh in church, but I seen them crack a smile or two during the service. Pa had tears in his eyes from laughing so hard.

Reverend Wells announced that the church needed some repairs and also some more room he thought If we put on an addition for the children's classroom and fixed the roof, the church should be good for a few more years.

Pa volunteered the lumber he said the pumpkins would pay for it. Asa would supply the hardware and windows and everyone else could help with labor.

The wagons from the produce company came this morning they got three loads today and the rest will be loaded Thursday that's a whole lot of pumpkins ten big wagons full, I'm glad we didn't have to load all of them.

Looks like we lost a couple dozen to deer and coons, but we still got enough for pie's and bread.

Me and Josh are going hunting in the morning we'll take Ralph with us to see how good he jumps deer, we just need enough meat for the party this week end. I'll grab a pig from the pen we'll roast it and a couple deer, that should be good for the meat.

The lumber for the church came in yesterday, we'll get to work on it first thing Monday morning, but first we have a cook-out to put on. We've been getting ready all week building tables and benches getting wood for the fire and making sure we have everything.

Ralph scared up a couple nice deer for us now we got all the meat we need,

Me and Josh skinned one of our pigs and the deer and Pa got the fire ready. Mom has been baking and cooking for three days now, looks like we're having potato-salad, cole' slaw, baked beans, green beans, rolls and cakes and pies along with the meat of course some of the guest's bring other dishes too, I think we'll have enough food for Josh. Pa got one of them ice-cream makers form Asa's store and he's been trying it out, it's frozen cream with berries and sugar sounds good.

Time to go get Linda now I'll drop Josh off at his house and pick him and Emily up on the way back.

When I got to Linda's she had a whole load of stuff to take to the party, we loaded everything and then she had to show me the new room they've been working on, It really looked good it surprised me how much work they done.

Asa had to ride to the party with us he was surprised how nice the coach was, he said he was going to order one to ride to church and back and maybe even do some traveling. Looks like there's plenty of people at the party already. I can smell the meat from here I guess the neighbors smell it too, that's how you invite everybody around here the smell in the air is all you need, no invitations needed.

Some of the men are playing horseshoes and the kids are running around playing and laughing, looks like Pas got a good crowd watching him make ice-cream, I think that will be a regular from now on.

Linda wore a real pretty white dress it looks like a wedding dress, I can barely keep my hands off her, I noticed she's attracting lots of attention, I feel like a million dollars beside her.

Reverend Wells gave the blessing and started the line for the food, he did a good job giving thanks for everything that we have accomplished in our community in the last few years, and all the good food here today.

Linda's eyes have a special glow tonight it makes me crazy when she looks into my eyes. She has the most beautiful auburn hair it goes all the way down her back and it's got just a little bit of curl to it.

Linda could have her choice of any man here but she picked me, I'm one lucky man, I hope I don't let her down.

Me and Linda plan on announcing our wedding tonight while everyone is here, I figure Josh and Lucy will do the same, I don't know about Bobby and Emily we'll see I guess. This will be our last get together before Christmas, hopefully we'll be married by then.

Pa got everybody's attention for a minute and asked me and Linda to come up, he said we have something to say.

It wasn't as hard as I thought it would be I guess everybody done figured out what we were going to say by now. I had one arm around Linda and I just said I'm the luckiest man in the country to be able to say, me and Linda are going to be married before the year is out and everyone is welcome to the wedding.

Lucy wasn't about to let the night go by without announcing their plans too, she done a really good job getting everybody's attention, yes my little sister was grown up now and she wanted us all to know it, Mom and Pa was trying to cover up their tears but I could tell they were proud of us both.

How about some ice-cream everybody Pa shouted trying to divert attention away from his feelings, It's some kind of good he said, especially with some warm apple pie I think Pa has started something with that ice cream maker, I bet Josh had three helpings. Asa said he's already got orders for six more ice cream makers just tonight.

Some new neighbors came by and introduced themselves as Tom and Nancy Bolling, they brought a guitar with em and sang songs all night, they had everybody there singing along.

Looks like everybody had a really good time tonight but now It's time to take Linda and the others home, tomorrow is Sunday and we've got church in the morning, and we still have to put up all this food tonight.

Bobby and Lucy can stay here and help Mom and Pa clean up and I'll take the others home. Josh wanted to drive home so me, Linda and Asa and Emily rode in the coach it's nice and cozy in there at night Asa was asleep before we got to Josh's house, we just let him sleep and I drove the rest of the way.

Seems like the weeks just fly by anymore I guess we better make good use of the time while we got it. Before you know it Linda and me will be getting married and raising kids and we'll be like Mom and Pa are now. That was my thoughts on the lonely ride home on the coach, I looked in the mirror when I got home and to my surprise I didn't have gray hair and wrinkles, I think I just need to slow down and try to take one day at a time.

Well it looks like we have plenty of help this morning on the church, I see Pete Allbright is here, he builds houses for a living, we should get this room built pretty fast.

Me and Pa started replacing shingles on the church roof, we've been noticing a puddle in the floor in front of the alter for a while now, every once in a while reverend Wells gets in just the right spot when he's preaching and that drip makes its way to his ear, believe me that changes the whole sermon.

Any ways me and Pa are about to put a stop to that old leak we got a whole bunch of extra cedar shakes with the lumber.

Some of the women are bringing food over later for lunch for everyone.

It's a good feeling when everyone gets together and does something for a good cause, If I had these men for a couple day's me and Linda could get our house built fast.

We're making benches for the kids to set on in the class room instead of buying them that will save us enough money to buy a new church bell.

Bill and Stan Lawson are laying stones for the new chimney, Asa ordered a nice, heavy, small stove for the classroom it should keep the kids warm for years to come.

Asa is one good man I'm going to like having him for my Father in Law and in our family. He lost his wife the same winter uncle Fred lost his. Linda was just a little girl then Asa raised her on his own and did a good job too, she can cook and clean and she can run the store good as Asa can.

Some of the women brought their young children with them, the little ones that ain't in school yet, they're helping gather hickory and chestnuts, I like to watch the kids when they pick up the prickly chestnuts, we all like the native nuts and berries. The women make candy and cakes and pies with them and that's some of my favorite reasons I like this time of year.

Pa has his mind set on a new tractor Asa showed him one in the catalog he's got and Pa's been talking about it ever since. The tractor is made of steel and it don't need horses, it runs on wood, and it sup-pose to take place of four or five horses, I got to see that thing.

It's about to get dark on us we'll have to finish the room tomorrow, at least we got the roof done if it rains tomorrow, we can work inside.

When we got home, Mom had some news for us, she waited till we all got to the table and announced she was going to have a baby. Pa's first words were, are you sure?

"I guess I aught to know I've had four of em" Mom said.

Pa tried to show he was happy with the news and said he was going to need some more kids cause all his were growing up and getting married.

Lucy said "don't worry Pa we'll be around all the time."

"I said sure Pa you won't even know we're gone." besides I don't know if I'm ready to stop eating Moms cooking yet.

Soup beans, cornbread, fried potatoes and fat back fried up crispy, and pumpkin pie with fresh cream on top for dessert, that always hits the spot after a long day's work. That bed is going to feel good tonight.

The next morning, I got up and helped Pa feed the stock, looks like we got rid of the varmints for now anyway.

I got two dozen eggs this morning Pa got us a pail of fresh cold milk from the cooler box, it keeps the milk cold all year round for us, it's just a block of ice with straw around it but it works. Asa gets the ice in once a week from up north somewhere. We plan on digging a cave near the creek to put ice in some day, it just seems there is always something else that needs done first.

Pa's been trying to get Mom to slow down some now that she's pregnant, but she's so used to hard work that she don't know how to slow down. Pa said he don't want to have to hog- tie her to get her to get some rest but if thats what it takes he will.

Me and Pa picked Josh up and headed to Asa's we needed some metal flashing for the chimney, it keeps the roof from leaking around the chimney. We want to get some of them sausages for lunch today.

It's cloudy this morning maybe we can get the roof done before it rains.

Asa got a real nice chalk board for the class room and some new felt erasers.

Everybody sat around drinking coffee and making plans for the day, Me and Pa went up to finish the roof before the rain comes.

This bunch of good neighbors we have will come to help anybody, whenever you need them all you have to do is holler.

We finished the roof and started on the front door. Any kid would be proud to have class in this classroom, I'd like to have it for a house.

The church ain't the only thing that needs work, our school is too small now also, we had three more families move in last summer and they all got kids.

We stopped by Asa's on the way home he said the tractor is on the way, should be here in about four days. Pa is excited as a kid at Christmas. Linda's coming home with us to learn some of Mom's cooking tricks, that's fine with me the more time I can spend with her the better.

We're going to have a celebration Sunday for the new addition, the Reverend will bless the room and the builders and we'll have a good meal after Sunday service.

Reverend Wells also wanted to remind everybody to check with their friends and make sure they have enough food and wood for the winter. We do this every year ever since the first year when we lost four people to the winter weather.

The snow can put a stop to everything for weeks at a time so it's better to be prepared for it.

I got to have my pick of dinners from Mom and Linda's cooking class, meatloaf or Elk roast I picked roast.

We got a new neighbor a couple weeks ago Giles Nash and his wife Betty, they have two kids school age. He's been studying to be a dentist Lord knows we need one here. We've been letting doc Jenkins do our teeth pulling and he's a horse doctor, I know most of the men around here would rather go to the black smith.

Randy Sparks is one of the rich kids around here he got a bicycle the other day, it's like a horse but it has wheels and it's not easy to ride on a rough road. Just look at Randy you can see the scars.

We'll be celebrating Thanksgiving soon, most of the leaves are off the trees and the fields are dried up and brown. The squirrels and the birds are busy gathering their food for winter. That's what most everyone around is doing too, making sure the woodsheds are full and the smokehouses are full and secure from the bears and wolves.

The mine helped us out a lot that's how we could afford to plant the pumpkins this year, and get the new plow and our horse Red, and everything else we got extra this year.

Me and Pa's going to Asa's this morning the tractor is in, and it gives me a chance to see Linda.

Looks like there's a crowd at the store I guess everybody wants to see the tractor.

The iron horse looks heavy and a lot bigger than I thought it would be, It looks like it can plow some ground, there's steam coming out of it in a couple different places and it makes sounds like a giant teapot boiling.

Pa wants to hook a plow to Red and one to the tractor and see which one can plow faster.

The men were putting bets on the tractor as we hooked up the plows, the same size plows, one on a horse the other on a tractor, Pa got the plow with Red and Tim Byler got on the tractor, since he had used one before. I got in front of em and Waved my handkerchief for the signal to go, Red dug in and the dirt was flying, you could see the muscles bulge out in his chest and legs, he jumped ahead and then the tractor dug in and didn't even slow down. Red went about thirty or forty feet and plowed up the ground like a pro. Pa stopped and looked back to watch the tractor it took about five minutes longer than Red did but he was breathing hard and the tractor was ready to go.

I would rather see the tractor do the hard work than Red, he can do it but it's much easier for the machine to do it.

Pa was impressed with Red and the tractor, looks like he'll be getting one next spring. We'll leave this one here for people to see in case they want to get one. Linda made some lemonade for everyone and passed around some of her home- made chocolate candy with fresh walnuts in it, some of the guys were calling me a lucky man you got a pretty girl and she can make good candy too.

Linda done ordered her dress for the wedding she showed it to me in a catalog it sure will be pretty on her, she could wear a feed sack and she would still look good.

It's hard to buy for a girl when her daddy owns a store, she's done got everything in the store, I'm going to take one of them catalogs home and try to find her something for Christmas that she ain't already got.

I'm going to make our wedding rings with some of our silver I've already got the instructions from the black smith on how to make them. I'll most likely have to help Josh and Bobby make theirs too. It's not that we can't afford to buy our rings but we have the silver, and it means more to someone when it's handmade.

First let's get over Thanksgiving, just two weeks away Me and Josh plan on going hunting Saturday, thought we'd go up on the north ridge they've been a lot of elk spotted there lately.

Josh said Ralph has been running off somewhere almost every day for a week now but he always comes back before dark, I told him Ralph probably has a girl- friend somewhere, and he's just like us he wants to go see her.

We got up early and set off hunting Ralph came with us and we kept him close by so he wouldn't spook the elk. We crossed over Stuart's creek and started up the north ridge when we jumped some deer but we really wanted some elk so we let them go.

The leaves are almost all off the trees and they're still soft so they don't make much noise when you walk on them. We will have to camp out tonight so we can be in the right spot early tomorrow morning, there's still a couple more hours of daylight left but we are close enough to set up camp we don't want to get too close to where they bed down, they will smell our fire.

Going to be a cold night but we found a good spot with a hill to block off the wind, I brought a tent from Asa's store they came from the army, Asa bought a bunch of surplus stuff after the big war years ago.

This tent makes it real nice beats sleeping in the open when it's cold out.

We got a couple rabbits on the way up here and I brought a sack of biscuits from the house, that should make a good supper for us.

I can hear some hoot owls nearby it's a real peaceful sound, along with the sound of leaves blowing around and a crisp wind whistling in the night air.

Me and Josh talked for a while as we ate supper, Josh asked about our lives when were married and wondered if we would still go hunting together like we always have, I told him we probably won't have the time like we do now but things won't change that much.

Ralph started growling and woke us up we heard something outside, I turned the lantern up and grabbed my gun and told Josh to hold Ralph.

I threw back the door flap on the tent just in time to see the backside of a huge bear, I didn't want to shoot a bear way out here so I shot in the air a couple times and the bear took off running, them things can run when they want to. I watched it until it was out of sight and then went back inside.

Josh was wide awake now and so was I, if Ralph so much as makes a sound I'm out the door with my rifle.

I don't think either of us got much sleep we ate a cold breakfast and took off hunting we left everything set up in case we have to stay another night.

The bear put a new sense of caution on our minds as we stalked our prey, every little sound is amplified now. If a bear got as close to us as that one did last night you wouldn't have much time to shoot before it would be right on you, and it would be all over but the crying.

Finally, a nice size Buck drinking from a creek about fifty yards away Josh let me take the first shot, the Elk didn't even jump it just fell right there. Now we need to hurry up and get it gutted and get out of here before the blood smell attracts another bear.

There's a whole lot of meat on a full- grown Elk, we had to work fast to get out of there and get back to safety. We had to make some drag poles to get all the meat out in one trip.

Ralph helps take the bears off our minds we've got all we can handle dragging the Elk. Any sound and Ralph's stopping and looking in that direction.

We'll go back to camp and eat some loin, before we pack up and head back, I don't want to stay here tonight with all this meat, the farther we get away from here the safer I'll feel. I told Josh. He agreed on the long walk back home, we got a chance to talk about the changes to come soon, Josh wants Lucy to live with him and his Mom and Pa's at least for a while. Emily will be gone soon with Bobby and they will stay at our place for now, and me and Linda will be at Asa's place.

We decided to take one day at a time, as long as we're with our girls everything would work out.

As time goes by it steals little pieces of our youth, and leaves us a little bit wiser, and a little older.

Now Christmas has come to our village and we are celebrating one very important Birthday along with three weddings. we all decided to let Christmas be extra special for all of us every year. We are having a triple wedding in our little church during our Christmas celebration.

The girls all look beautiful in their white gowns, I can see what Josh see's in Lucy now my little sister grew up fast.

Emily looks grown up too and she's as pretty as a picture. Linda takes my breath away I can't begin to tell you how she looks to me.

Me and Josh look to be nervous but Bobby is cool as a cucumber for some reason, I hope Josh don't pass out before the preacher gets done.

The rings we made from the silver look really good, the girls thought they were store- bought.

Mom is all dressed up and she's starting to show some, but Mom always looks good Pa looks nice too in his new suit from back east.

Losing three kids all at the same time probably is hard for Mom and Pa but they still got one little girl, Suzy and she'll be around for a long the time at least another ten years.

We all lined up, boys on one side and girls on the other then the preacher started the ceremony, I got a lump in my throat and the sweat was rolling down my face I looked around at Josh he's green and shaking like a leaf, the preacher said relax boys this will only take a minute.

It was the longest five minutes of my life, I really don't remember all the words just the last ones, you may kiss the bride, I thought I would pass out but I made it.

About that time somebody shouted out it's snowing we all ran out to see the Christmas snow. It's not like we haven't seen snow this year, there's just something about Christmas and snow and children laughing and playing.

The kids started singing carols and most everyone there joined in, it sounded like one of them recording things like Asa has in the store that you wind up and music comes out of it I think we'll remember this Christmas for a long time.

We all ate Christmas dinner, ham, Elk and just about any food you can think of and we had eggnog with fruitcake and plumb pudding and every kind of dessert too.

Mom and Pa never taught us much about the birds and the bees, I think we'll figure it out though.

Asa said he wouldn't let anyone disturb us tonight and we could sleep as long as we want.

I won't go into any details but, I could not explain in a million years how wonderful I feel with Linda by my side now. It's the look Mom and Pa gives each other, it puts a twinkle in your eyes and a smile on your face that won't go away.

After our three day, honeymoon we rode Asa's horse drawn sleigh through the snow to Moms for Sunday supper.

The house was full of the faces that would forever be a part of this family.

There are so many smiles around the table it looks like somebody told a funny story or something.

Mom and the girls made a real nice meal for us, ham with honey and apple slices on it, mashed potatoes, green beans rolls and fresh apple pie and rhubarb pie and Pas ice cream.

After we ate supper Mom took the girls in her bedroom to talk about girl stuff, and pa did the same with us. He wanted to know if we had any questions about being married or anything else. I asked him when would we stop smiling like this. He said Son if you're lucky you never will, he said that's happiness and I hope all of you feel that for the rest of your lives. Whenever you need anything at all come to me, Asa or Tom if we can't help you then you don't need help.

Pa wanted to let us know he wanted to go to the mine before Spring planting time, we should have the claims papers soon and he would like to get it staked.

Pa had to show off his new fly rod Mom got him for Christmas, he's real proud of it.

It seems like time stands still until you look back and then you think it flies, now January has come and gone without so much as a howdy or a goodbye.

We got the papers in for the claim on the mine Pa and Asa have been reading it to try and understand everything. Asa assures us it's legal for us to claim if it is not already staked.

Pa wants to go this Saturday I hate to leave Linda this soon but we need to make sure nobody gets there before us. Uncle Fred and Josh and me and Pa will be going Bobby is needed at the store. Pa told the girls to keep an eye on Mom and don't let her work too hard.

I told Linda she had Lucy and Emily to keep her company while I was gone and they were all sisters now they should take care of each other and this would be the last time I would go without her.

Mom made us some country ham and biscuits and gravy for breakfast, we had some pumpkin pie for dessert.

It's cold this morning but it's clear, I didn't want to leave Linda, all of a sudden I had this lonely feeling in my gut when I realized it would be almost two weeks before I would see her again, Pa could see it on my face, he said don't worry son you have the rest of your lives to be together, she'll be just fine with your mom and the girls.

We brought along a small stove and a tent that Asa got from the army surplus some time ago, and some dry fire wood. We set the tent up on the wagon and made a fire in the stove, it was really nice and warm in the tent you could fall asleep easy.

Uncle Fred had never been more than a couple miles west of his place till now, I was telling him about the trees and the big rabbits, you could see the excitement in his eyes, especially when I told him you could build five houses with just one tree.

Me and Josh slept for a long time before Fred woke us up to eat lunch, we just stayed in the wagon and ate stopping only long enough to feed and water the horses. Pa and Uncle Fred sat up front with the tent flap opened up where the warm air could reach their backs they just kept on driving.

After a few more naps It started getting dark, Pa stopped under some trees for the night.

Me and josh fixed some ham on the stove and heated up some bread and made some coffee, it was almost like being at home.

Pa and Fred drove all day while me and Josh slept, now we're wide awake, but it's too dark to keep going so we have to stay here.

The hay we brought for the horses make a good bed with a blanket over it, almost as good as mine at home.

Every time I think of home, I have to see if I'm dreaming, I just got married a few weeks ago but it don't seem real, it seems like just yesterday Mom is waking me up to get ready for school and I'm telling her, just five more minutes I'll be there and Bobby's got the covers all pulled over to his side of the bed and we're playing tug of war until I get up.

The smell of bread as it's browning and bacon and gravy is what always woke me up. Now Linda and me are together and Mom's not here to get me up I'll have to learn to get up and help Linda fix breakfast if I'm going to eat.

The next thing I knew it was morning, I was dreaming about all this stuff, How I could still sleep? I don't know after sleeping all day, Guess I lost a lot of sleep the last few weeks.

Josh had already been hunting and Pa was frying up a couple big fat rabbits to go with some fresh biscuits he'd just made.

After that delicious breakfast we set off for the mine again, well rested and bellies full we would make our way west at a gallop, the ground was frozen with a couple inches of snow on top, which made for a good ride. The further we rode the deeper the snow got.

I shot a small deer around mid-day and we stopped to clean it and eat lunch while we rested the horses.

Back on the trail we could see rabbit tracks, deer tracks, lots of turkey tracks and small game more than we are use to seeing back home.

Uncle Fred noticed as far as you can see there are no signs of man, and that's a good thing he said. You don't need to worry about the mine.

The snow was a couple feet deep now but it was powdery and blowing. Pa said "See that mountain way up ahead there Fred? That's where we're headed.

Uncle Fred squinted his eyes, and said "I don't see nothing."

The mountain was still half a day away but it seems almost in touch now.

Pa noticed the snow was now rubbing the bottom of the wagon floor, we worried about it getting deeper.

Pa gave the reins a whip and yelled "git up Red!" and the wagon rolled a little faster.

Pa said he would like to get there before dark and the extra speed will help keep the horses warm.

At last we get to the campsite at the foot of the mountain, me and Josh put up a cover for the horses gave them food and water then gathered some fire wood, while Pa and Fred got supper ready.

Pa made some really good corn fritters along with the deer loin and fried onion and taters.

Uncle Fred looks like he's gaining some weight to me I told Josh.

Josh said"At least he'll be able to buy some new clothes that fits when we get back home."

Josh don't say much but when he does it's always funny.

Uncle Fred has begun to open up to us a little he was so quiet now he's telling stories about Mom and him in the old country and the early years in America. Some of the stories about Ireland don't sound too happy and the look on Fred's face tells the story itself'.

Mom was a few years younger than Fred so she didn't get to see much hardship except for the hard times she faced at home. I couldn't imagine life being that bad, Mom never would tell us about those times, I guess it hurt too much not knowing what become of her folks.

I dreamed of me and Linda in the old country, though we were always hungry we were happy just being together. We had two kids and could barely feed them, so we sent them to America on a ship, and before they landed in the new land Pa was waking me up with the smell of fried deer meat and fresh coffee. Wow that was hard just to dream about it much less live it.

Fred said most of the people on the ship stayed in Boston and got jobs and places to stay, that's where your Mother met your Father and they stayed there and worked for a couple years I guess, I met Alice on the wagon train headed west. We had some good years together, till the winter of sixty- eight I think it was, she just wasn't strong enough to make it through that winter. After that I swore I wouldn't take another Wife unless I was sure I could take care of her. All these years I've just been getting by feeling sorry for myself and living day to day.

Pa said "Fred you don't have to explain to us we know how you feel about the past. This is going to be a new start for all of us and you are part of this family from now on, Ralph went over and put his paw on Fred's leg, just like he knew what we were saying, that made us all smile. Fred said "Pass one of them biscuits over here." then we all laughed.

It was cold outside of the warm tent and we had a long climb ahead of us. We put drag poles behind the horses and loaded them down with supplies then led them up the mountain. The trees kept most of the snow trapped in their foliage above and out of the woods so it wasn't that slippery climbing the mountain, yet in no way was it easy.

Pa tried to keep us moving, whistling that same old lull'aby he always uses, I guess Fred knew it too cause they both started in. It seemed to help take your mind off of the climb for a while. We stopped to eat lunch and rest our legs about half-way up the mountain, Fred couldn't help looking up at the trees, trying to see the tree tops that were surrounded by clouds, I told him it was easier to see if he lay on his back, my neck was sore for two days from looking up the first time I was here.

Pa said if we're going to get their before dark we had better get going. Then he started his whistling again.

The mountain gets really steep at one place and you have to be careful not to lose your footing or you could be starting the climb all over again.

Uncle Fred wants to take some seedlings from the big trees back with us to plant on his place, good idea I said.

We had to use lanterns the last hour of our climb the sun had already left us in the dark.

Josh took Ralph to flush out some birds just before dark, they got some nice pheasants for supper.

When we got to the cave, we looked for signs of strangers but didn't see any. Uncle Fred was impressed with the drawings as well as the silver in the walls. He said "How in the world did you boys find this place?" I don't see anybody ever finding it.

We set the tent up at the cave entrance then started a fire outside the tent to fix the birds, then we put the stove in the tent. Me and josh gathered more firewood while Pa and Fred tried to make out the drawings. Uncle Fred says he will make copies of the drawings to take back with us to show some people he knows. We all agree they're Indian drawings, but what does it mean.

Pa fixed the pheasants on the open fire and made some biscuits on the stove, that was some good eating.

Pa said we should carve our name on the cave entrance along with the claims stake, He would carve S&B Mining Co. On the face of the cave before we left.

Ralph got his own bird for supper since he jumped em up, I think he likes Pheasant I told Josh. He said I ain't seen anything he don't like yet.

Uncle Fred is right at home here, he looks happier than I've ever seen him. I think he's ready to get back to living.

We listened to some more tales of the old country while we ate supper and I fell asleep somewhere in Ireland a long time ago.

I was walking down a country road in the spring of the year the smell of fresh flowers in the air, I looked around and the most beautiful auburn- haired, green- eyed angel you could possibly imagine was standing there right in front of me. I couldn't talk I could only move my lips, but no sound came from my mouth. I was trying to say Linda, but she was walking away from me, the more I tried to speak the further away she got.

Then Ralph came over and licked me awake, right in the ear.

Pa and Fred were already chipping away at the mine, Josh was eating breakfast by himself, he figured I might want to eat so he sent Ralph over to wake me up.

I found myself looking around from time to time, hoping to catch a glimpse of the girl in my dream, it seemed so real.

I found Pa and Uncle Fred digging away, whistling just as happy as could be.

"Where you been Son? We just about got a load already." Pa said.

"You should have got me up." I said

"The way you were talking in your sleep I was afraid to." he said

"Come on and grab a pick we want to be finished digging before dark."

We left Josh to the hunting and wood gathering before coming to help us.

Fred knows more about silver than we do he's tried his hand at prospecting before he said, and this is some of the best ore he ever seen, and it looks like the vein we're working on goes deeper into the mountain it should hold out for a long time.

Pa said you boys keep on digging I'm going to mark our name on the entrance and put our claim number on the wall, just to make everything legal.

Josh just got back from hunting, he had to get food for the night and for breakfast tomorrow.

Josh said he saw some bear tracks not too far away from our camp so we need to be on alert tonight.

Me, Josh and Uncle Fred kept on digging till lunch time, Pa had some squirrels cooked up, he makes some unbelievable squirrel gravy.

Pa had the name for the mine carved overhead when we came out, S&B Mining Co. In big letters is what it read, with the claim number 952 right beside the name.

That makes me feel much better he said everything is all legal now, we all have to sign the papers when we get back and it's done. He said them letters are for Smith and Barton Josh, half of it belongs to you and the other half is Wills.

Pa's squirrel gravy really hit the spot, not many people get to eat this good on the trail, and some don't eat this good at home.

"How much more digging you think we got to do Fred?" Pa asked

Fred told him "Two more bags should finish this load I figure."

"Yeah Pa that's what I figure too." I said

"We're in a good thick streak right now it don't take long to get a load, some of it is almost pure, hardly any rock at all."

"That's sounds good men, three or four more hours and we'll get a good night's rest and start down first thing in the morning."

Pa said "It's too easy to break a leg going down tonight."

We filled the last two bags of ore and got everything ready to load in the morning.

Fred made drawings of the cave walls while Pa got supper ready, me and Josh fed the horses and gathered enough fire wood for the night.

We all settled down for a good meal, Pa gave thanks for our good fortune and good health, and the safety of our families before we began eating.

These dreams of mine are really working on me, I don't know what to expect next, And Pa says I've been talking in my sleep, hope I don't say nothing bad. One thing for sure I don't think I'll go anywhere overnight without Linda again.

I can hear the cold wind blowing outside and it makes me smile knowing I'm in this nice warm tent, I pull my blanket up to my chin and fall asleep.

Sometime in the night another dream came to me Linda, Emily, Lucy and Mom were all pregnant at the same time, and Linda and me already have two kids, Bobby and Emily have three and Josh and Lucy have two.

I remember looking in the mirror in our new house near the mine, I noticed my hair was gray, I looked at my hands and they were old and worn with wrinkles. I'm thinking, time sure does fly about that time Pa is shaking me to get up.

"Wake up Son it's almost daylight." he said.

I looked around and they were all three watching me sleep. They said I was talking about getting old or something. Thank the lord I'm still young it was all just a dream.

Pa said he thinks we should use drag poles on the horses to take some of the load off their backs, so we got some nice strong cedar poles and strapped them to the horses, loaded them down with hefty loads of ore, and It seemed to do the job.

The drag poles help a lot but it's still hard to hold the horses back going down the mountain, Pa and Fred found out just how hard.

After about an hour we switched places to give them a rest the hardest part of the hill was behind us now, but it was still hard work.

Me and Josh got a chance to show Pa we could handle the horses and let him see that we are not young boys anymore.

The two older men were watching close for a while then settled in to a relaxed mood after seeing the young men take control of the animals.

"If I knew you could handle the horses going down this mountain I would have let you hours ago." Pa said.

Fred said "These boys grew up in the last couple of years, its time to give them the reins and let go Tom."

"I guess your right Fred, It's hard to believe how fast they grow up ain't it."

By the time we got to the half way point of the journey, we had to stop and rest, this was the heaviest load yet and the horses showed it. A rock had cut Reds left front leg and it was bleeding just a little bit.

Fred looked at it and said "josh do you remember seeing any willows around here?"

"Sure back there where the stream is." Josh replied.

"What about some oak moss?" Fred asked.

"Right over there is some." I said.

We got the backwoods medicine for Uncle Fred and he put the willow- bark-juice on Reds ankle, covered it with the moss then wrapped a rag around it. He said "leave it on the rest of the way he should be o k in a day or two."

We checked our other horse for cuts, and he looked o k, so we got our food out and had some lunch, I gave the horses some grain as a treat for the hard work.

Fred took advantage of our break to dig some sprouts from the giant trees, to take home and plant on our farms. He must have got four or five dozen sprouts, when my kids are my age they should be able to climb these sprouts.

Me and Josh led the horses the rest of the way down the mountain while Pa and Fred tried to clear the way for us, we finally got to our camping spot with a little touch of light left, we set up the tent, built a fire and unloaded the horses, before settling down for the night.

"I don't know about you but I'm beat." I told Josh.

You and me brother, I just want to eat and go to sleep."

Pa said "You boys done a man's job today, and I'm proud of both of you, maybe this ham and gravy and biscuits will help you sleep."

I don't remember closing my eyes, all I know is me and Linda were in our barn at our new house trying to doctor on our horses leg and all of a sudden Uncle Fred shows up and takes over. He said you kids go on in I'll take care of this.

We went in the house and Mom had fixed cookies and lemonade with the kids as a surprise for us, when we got back.

Mom was there and Bobby and Lucy and little Suzy was grown up now and she was talking to some young man that I didn't know.

About the time I was getting ready to eat one of the fresh home made walnut cookies, Pa was shaking my foot to wake me up, I was telling him about Suzy being all grown up and he said wait just a minute there I done lost three kids this year already don't go getting Suzy married off too.

I asked how long had I been sleeping, Fred said we let you sleep about half an hour, I figured you would want to get back home as soon as you could.

I couldn't tell if I was asleep ten minutes or ten hours with these crazy dreams I've been having.

Back to the trail Pa and Fred took the reins for a while, that gave me and Josh a chance to hunt some more of them big squirrels, just one of em' had as much meat as a chicken.

We went on ahead and got two nice squirrels and a nice fat pheasant for supper tonight. Me and Josh had the game all skinned and cleaned by the time Pa and Fred got to us. We took over the reins and let them rest a while.

When we got to the campsite at the base of the mountain we noticed some of ground had been scraped and dug out, Pa noticed some bear tracks leading off to the east but nothing seemed to be broken, so we set up the tent and started a fire.

I could see the bear from the last hunting trip me and Josh went on up at the North Ridge, that was a big bear.

"I guess we'll be on high alert tonight men." Pa said

"Josh keep a close eye out while I'm fixen supper the bear might want to join us."

Josh looks all around like an old barn owl in every direction, and says "Yes sir."

The moon was out and shining bright the wind was blowing from west to the east so I knew the bear could probably smell the squirrels on the fire. I took my new rifle and went down to the creek to fill the water cans and canteens. Off in the distance on the other side of the creek I noticed something big moving but I couldn't see it too good, it was almost dark now. I set the cans down and held up my lantern to get a better look when he stood up, it was a grizzly and a big one too. The best I could tell he was looking right at my lantern, I yelled out beaar! And set the lantern down I didn't want to take my eyes off the bear, I cocked my rifle and waited for him to move, Josh, Pa and Uncle Fred showed up right as he started toward me. I just aimed for his eyes and pulled the trigger, he was still coming at me when Josh shot him, he still didn't go down, Pa seen what was going on and he shot the bear too. This time the giant of a bear came down and landed half in the creek and half out, It took me a while to stop shaking, and I still wouldn't take my eyes off the bear for some time, wanting to make sure it didn't get back up.

Pa says"I sure hope his buddies don't come for a visit tonight."

I wanted to laugh but I just couldn't I bet you could smell the fear on me.

We waited another ten minutes or so and went to check the bear out, Just like everything else around here the bears are huge too.

"Well it looks like we got some skinning to do tonight."Pa said

Josh was still looking around like an owl with his gun cocked and ready.

We couldn't have picked a better spot to shoot the bear the stream made clean up easy.

Uncle Fred said the bear would weigh eight hundred pounds cleaned. Pa said it would go every bit of one thousand pounds with the hide too. Any ways we got a lot of bear meat to take home with us. There was three bullet holes right between the bears eyes when we checked him.

Ralph had been acting funny and growling earlier so we tied him to a tree before we built the fire, If he got to that bear he'd be a gon'er. Yeah we got lucky I could have been bent over getting water when the bear started across the stream.

"I'm just glad its over I'll sleep better tonight now." Pa says

"Me too but I still don't think I'll sleep much." I said

"Come on boys lets get the drag poles and Red and get this back to the camp."Pa said

There was plenty of snow on the ground so we covered the bear meat with as much snow as we could, then we spread the hide out on the ground to look at it, we could cover the whole floor of the tent with the giant fur, it would be a trophy in my house, whenever I get one and a warning to us all of the dangers that the new world could bring us if we're not prepared.

We ate squirrel for supper, while trying to figure out how everything grows so big in the west, and wondering what we may run into next.

I was afraid to try to sleep in fear of getting eaten by a bear, with the dreams I had been having lately feeling so real, the bear scared me enough already.

While I sat there like an Indian with a blanket around me trying not to dose off, I could see I wasn't the only one worried about falling asleep. Josh was half awake all night and Pa and Uncle Fred didn't get much sleep either.

Pa fixed some bear meat for breakfast with gravy and biscuits, I had forgotten how good the beef like meat was.

Pa said "Get use to it we got half a ton of it to eat."

"Asa could sell some for us if need be." I said

Fred said "the new families could use some, that's a whole lot of meat."

"Looks like we're going to have a extra heavy load on the wagon, I hope it can handle it." Pa said

"You guys look like you didn't get much sleep last night, I knew you couldn't sleep so you would be watching out, and I could get some sleep, so I'll drive and let you all sleep a while.

I fell asleep listening to Pa whistling that Irish lullaby that he always does when he's happy.

Nice and warm in the tent on the wagon with the blanket pulled up to my neck I was soon dreaming again.

Once again me and Linda are out hunting when we come upon a cute bear cub, Linda has to go over and pet the little fellow I didn't think it was a good idea but when she's happy I'm happy. I told her the mother had to be close by and we should leave it alone. We started walking off but the little cub just kept following us. Then I hear a growl the cub stops and turn around to see his momma bear and runs to her, while Me and Linda sneak off behind some trees, Then I wake up sweating and breathing heavy. Josh is still asleep and Pa and Fred are driving away.

"The snow is getting heavier by the minute. Pa tells Us and it's getting hard to see the trail, we don't want to break a wheel in a chug-hole."

The ground was frozen that helped to keep the wagon from sinking into the ground, and the snow acted as a cushion to make for a smooth ride.

We had to stop every mile or so to clean the snow from the tarp on the wagon, and the snow only got harder as we traveled east.

Pa said it looked like the sun was trying to come out and the snow was slowing down some, so that's good news.

We made it to the outcrop of large rocks we named Buffalo rock for its noticeable shape and decided to stay there over night, if we pull up on the right side of the rock it will block the weather from two sides pretty good.

It felt good to have all those miles behind us and the large bears too hopefully.

The moon was really bright tonight, you could see for miles when the snow wasn't coming down.

I could hear the wind as it blows against the Buffalo shaped rocks, almost sounding like the moaning of the Buffalo's as it curls around the rocks edges. Still glad to be in the warm wagon with the cold wind only to be heard and not felt, I fall asleep again.

The new day brings us sunshine and heavy winds, we put side blinders on the horses to keep some weather out of their eyes but there's only so much we can do for them.

The cold temperatures would keep the bear meat fresh the whole trip and feed us all the while.

Three days later we pull into the barn at the home place and were greeted by our girls, like we were gone for years, and tears of joy would run down all of our cold faces.

We showed everyone the bear hide and it would send chills down your back, knowing how big the beast really was.

Now with these weeks of separation behind us we can get back to our freshly started lives together.

We were not the only ones with news, Mom told us the best she could tell, at least two of the girls were pregnant along with her. Linda and Emily were going to have children but Lucy showed no signs so far.

"You mean I'm going to be a father?" I said

"Looks that way son, how's it feel?" Pa asked

"I don't know, It hit me so fast let me set down a minute." I murmured.

The dream that I had on the mountain is coming true.

I went to the kitchen to look in the mirror, to see if I was gray headed yet, I didn't see any gray hairs, but I felt older just knowing I'm going to be a father.

Linda wanted to go home, so we got Josh and Lucy and headed to Asa's. I dropped Josh and Lucy off and me and Linda went to our new home.

Asa was all ears as we both gave him our news, I told him about the grizzly but all he wanted to hear was about the baby. He's already talking about getting him this or that and the baby aint even here yet.

He said this might be his only chance to spoil a grandchild, and he plans on doing it right.

I was about to fall asleep so me and Linda went on to bed, It sure felt good to be back with her, two weeks felt like two months.

I made her a promise not to stay away from her overnight again, and I plan on keeping that promise.

We got back on Saturday so we will be eating at Mom and Pa,s house tomorrow, celebrating the new babies and the trip to the mine.

Mom fixed bear-pot-roast for supper with cornbread and pumpkin-strawberry cupcakes for dessert, Mom could make dirt taste good, that pot roast was delicious.

While we were eating Lucy had to get up and throw up her supper. Mom asked her if the meat made her sick, She just said she had been feeling sick for a couple days now, and didn't think it was the food.

Mom and Pa just looked at each other with that look, like only they knew what was going on, and they were.

One of our new neighbors came to the front door while we were eating, he was carrying a puppy, the cutest little feller you ever seen.

He asked for the one that owns that red dog that's been coming over to his place lately. Ralph was under the table when Josh said "this dog?"

"Yeah that's him, this is one of his pups, our dog had seven of em about three weeks ago, he seems like a good dog I thought you might want one of em."

Josh said "I knew he was up to something staying gone so long every day."

"How many are you going to keep?" I asked, while remembering we didn't even know his name.

Pa introduced us all to the man and he said his name was Earl Matney, he moved in down next to the Yates' in July, it's just me and my wife Pearl.

Pa said "Sue fix him a bowl of pot roast and give him a chair."

Earl said "No thanks, my wife had supper ready when I left, but I do thank you."

"You got plenty food and wood for the winter Earl?" Pa asked

He said some of the men from church brought him some last week, and he really was thankful for it. It looks like a good place to settle down he said.

He said he was going to keep one of the pups but the rest would be weened in a couple weeks, he just wanted to give us first picks cause we had the daddy.

I said "I believe we might take one." Then Bobby, and Pa wants one for Suzy and Uncle Fred said "If they're anything like Ralph I'll take one."

The weeks came and went and life in the Idaho frontier went along too. Come to find out Lucy had morning sickness it wasn't the roast at all, Mom had a little boy in March and named him after Pa, Thomas Robert Smith.

Me and Lucy had a boy in August, we named him Asa, his grandfather is so proud of him, if we could just keep him from buying him so much stuff.

Josh and Lucy had a girl in September her name is Kerry.

And Bobby and Emily had twin boys in September, Peter and Paul.

Someone once told me Time sure does fly, and I reckon he was right.

The mine is being run by some company from California, they pay us once a month and we have eyes on the place all the time Uncle Fred sees to that. The mountain is not to be disturbed on the outside.

Me and Lucy have plans to move next year. Asa is going to let Bobby have the store so he can move west with us, that's one way to keep him from spoiling little Asa.